Stuffed

By Sylvia Morrow

For detailed content notes please visit the authors website at SylviaMorrow.com.

The author will happily answer any further questions via her social media inboxes. Just be warned, she's a chatterbox!

Chapter 1

Anne

"Holy shit, dude, ever hear of personal space?"

I dodge some creep on the sidewalk who walks way too close, nearly brushing up against me. He looks sweaty and grimy. I shudder as I walk away from him. That was way too close of a call.

After some fancy footwork, I make it up the busy sidewalk without touching anyone. My apartment building is a relief to see. I know once inside, I'll nearly be to my little place where I can be all alone, just how I like. I open the front door to the building, only to bump chest first into Jimmy, my landlord.

"Hey there, little Annie. You got your rent? Or you gonna make me come get it from you?" Jimmy winks a glassy blue eye at me.

I back away, my hands itching to toss off the jacket I'm wearing. I can't stand the idea of wearing something he touched. Being stuck with him is killing me.

"Rent isn't due for five days, Jimmy. I'll have it in by then. You know I always do."

"Never hurts to have a reminder though, right, girly?" He licks a worm-like bottom lip which sets my teeth on edge.

My fingers feel so itchy I start rubbing them against one another furiously. It's a tic I can't help doing when I get too upset or anxious. I used to have a lot more obvious tics, but I've worked on them over time through therapy. This particular one just stuck.

"Okay, see you later Jimmy," I say with a fake smile I really freaking struggle to put on. Thankfully he moves to the side so I can squeeze past and up to my apartment.

I slam and lock the door, throw off my clothes, and get into a hot shower where I scrub myself with antibacterial soap. Once I feel good and clean I get out and decide to have a nice night watching a show or two and just chilling. I'm admittedly a bit obsessed with anime but I'm not worried about it. Everyone has a hobby, plus it calms me down and I could really use some relaxation.

The butler character in the anime I'm watching tonight is fighting with a reaper in a scene I've seen a million times before. This is my favorite show. I watch this one like every other night. Some people might think it's weird that this character in particular gets me so physically excited but, well my body reacts, and it reacts *strongly*.

Now, I don't like *real* people. I really, really don't.

Aside from my small family and online friends, that is. Those particular folks are awesome because I don't have to *touch* them. I get to enjoy their presence platonically and from at least several inches away. But dating? Gross. My hooha dries up at the thought.

The industry I work in, game design, is overwhelmingly male. Even surrounded by men there aren't any I want. There are never any I want *anywhere*, and I'm glad about that because dating seems like the worst. It just doesn't appeal to me.

The thought of sweaty hands groping me, people's germs all over me...eew. I hate germs and touching, and sex is packed with nothing but bodily fluids and I can't think of anything worse.

But fictional characters are a whole other story.

I watch the colors move across the screen, clutching a pillow between my legs—my favorite pillow.

It's the perfect firmness, soft enough to lay my head on at night but firm enough to do this naughty thing I like to do. More like an embarrassing thing, actually. If anyone saw me, I think I would die, but it just feels so, so good. With my perfect pillow between my legs and my fictional boyfriend on the T.V., everything is just right in the world.

My satin pajama pants feel so smooth against my thighs, my ass...along my sensitive folds. They're already slick with the juices the animations have drawn from me tonight. I grip my pillow tighter, imagining it's the mysterious butler from the television, and sliding myself slowly up and down against it.

Fictophilia. That's what it's called when you're only attracted to fictional characters. I can't help it. Thinking of actual skin touching me is just repulsive. But this pillow between my thighs, riding it, is perfect for me. No skin, no germs, no potential for disease. Only stroking and grinding just right while thinking of my animated man.

I push harder against the pillow, letting the satin of these pink pajama pants slide against my slippery pussy. I'm really wet now, and I dip my hips against the pillow, opening my legs wide for a moment to slip along my core where I'm leaking for my butler.

My legs close tight as I grind as hard as I can against the pillow, soaking through my pants—and into the pillow itself at this point, I'm sure. My clit is forced against the layers of fabric, relentlessly ground against the firm block of feathers and cotton, over and over until my legs squeeze and shake. A silent scream forms in my mouth as my eyes close tight. My cunt spasms against the pillow; I come hard.

After my moment of release, I fall down onto the bed, relaxed, and pull the pillow up against my head. It's slightly moist but I don't care, I just flip it around. I'll change the case tomorrow. Right now, I'm exhausted.

I'm not sure if I'm actually a *fictophiliac*, or if it's just that I know I won't ever find anyone real I can be with. I guess it doesn't really matter either way. I like an orgasm as much as anyone, so yeah, it would be cool if there were some way for one of my beloved characters to help me out, but I'm sane enough to know that's not going to happen. My television, my imagination, and my favorite pillow will just have to do. After all, there's no way I'll ever have a real man to be with.

I set my glasses on the side table. The remote is within reach and I grab it, turning off the television.

"Goodnight my darling," I whisper into the dark.

As I'm falling asleep I swear I imagine I hear the same returned.

Chapter 2

Pillow

Oh Anne. Anne, my *darling*. My *wondrous* Anne.

She made use of me again tonight, and it was glorious. It had been ages since she'd gripped me tight and run me between her warm thighs. I was beginning to worry she had forgotten about me. I don't know what I would have done if that would have happened.

Anne is my reason for living. Well, if you could call what I'm doing now living, which I wouldn't. At this moment, I'm simply existing.

Though I was part of something alive once, I barely recall it. A phoenix, it was. Once upon a time, this phoenix—a powerful and ancient creature known for its ability to regenerate—fell in love with...a goose.

How disappointing. How uninspired.

You'd think a creature of legend would choose something more *interesting*, but I guess a phoenix is just a fancy bird when it all comes down to it.

And, well, to make a sad story short, the goose got cooked, so the phoenix died of sadness. Too heartbroken to be revived, it perished in a funeral pyre of its own making.

However, before it died, a single one of its feathers fell amidst the goose's own down. When the humans gathered them and stuffed them into their "organic, free range, all natural goose feather pillows" the phoenix feather got scooped up along with it.

And that's how my existence began.

In just one feather there is a tiny spark of regenerative power. A Phoenix can't come back from one feather alone—there's no *bird* left. There's no *anything* left in me, aside from the tiniest potential for life. I would have been only a feather in a pillow if it weren't for *her*. The passion she projected onto me added a bit of spark to the little flicker of life in the plume, just enough to give me awareness.

And to give me an aching desire for *Anne.*

On its own, it's not enough to give me a physical form. It's not enough to give me *Anne.* But ever so slowly, I'm building up more life, more mass, more energy, *more* for *her.*

Just now, a fly buzzes into Anne's room; this will be perfect if things go just right. I wait patiently to see where the insect will go. Not that I can wait any other way. After all, I'm an inanimate object.

The fly drops down onto Anne's head, all its disgusting legs touching her glorious mane of golden-brown hair. *How dare it touch her*. I wait as it flits about around the bed until, finally, it lands on *me*. It takes less than half a second for the fly to drop down, dead, and for me to feel a little more alive.

Alive. Someday I'll have enough life stored inside to turn myself into a creature Anne could love. She'll hold me, caress me, and I'll *feel* all of it and I'll give her every bit of pleasure she deserves.

As long as she doesn't give up on me, doesn't throw me away before then, of course.

I concentrate on using the energy I absorbed from the fly to keep my fabric cool, and my feathers fluffed just the way she likes them. To make sure she never throws me away, I need to remain perfect until I can become the man she needs. Because I know she *does* need me, and I need her. Things will be so wonderful when I'm *alive*.

Chapter 3

Anne

Finally, it's five o'clock and I can go home. Today has been the worst day at work. There were so many meetings, all of them in packed rooms where I was jammed next to tons of coughing, sweating, *leering*, people. I just want to take a shower, order some food, and relax. No people, no deadlines, just me and whatever I feel like watching tonight.

I start to smile as I pack my bag, thinking of the relaxing night ahead of me. Maybe even an upbeat night to wash away this negativity. I can put on some Sailor Scouts—fight the evil feelings by the moonlight.

Heck, I could even turn on the PC and play a game with my online friends. We could get the guild together and just nerd out. It's been way too long since I checked in on them, I should make sure they're okay. As I finish packing up, my budding smile turns to a frown as I think about how antisocial I've been with all the stress from work.

"Hey there, little miss grumpy."

The interruption shocks me from my thoughts, causing me to jump and spill the contents of my bag all over the floor. *Argh*, all my favorite Copic markers roll under the desk. Those things are expensive, and I'll be damned if I lose any of them. I close my eyes and take a deep breath, trying to calm myself before replying to the jerk who broke me away from my pleasant thoughts.

"What do you want, Todd?" I ask in a tone that admittedly does nothing to disprove his claim of my grumpiness.

"Just wanted to see if you'd be interested in going out with me tonight? We could go get some drinks, go back to my place, play some games…who knows what else? Could be fun, right?" Todd asks in his perpetually phlegmy voice.

He leans one bony shoulder against the wall of my cubicle and I can see the sweat stains under the arm of his vintage band t-shirt. One of his fingers trails along my forearm. I pull away. *No touching. No, no, no.* I begin to hurriedly pick up my scattered items, avoiding his gaze as much as possible.

"I'm not interested. I've told you already, I'm here to work, not find a date. Please respect that," I tell him, trying to retain my composure.

I tend to cry when I get upset and I don't want to do that. This is a professional environment, even though it doesn't seem like it half the time, and I'm the only woman working on this team. I can't be seen crying.

"You can do both, you know, Annie Banannie. In fact, I think it might even help your work to experience a little romance. Relax and let your mind free to new ideas or whatever." Todd brushes against my arm again and this time tears build in the corners of my eyes.

Please stop touching me.

I pack up the rest of my items and sling my bag over my shoulder. "No. End of it."

My jaw clenches as I walk out the door, fingertips frantically rubbing against one another. Todd scoffs behind me. I think tonight I'm not feeling fun or social after all. Watching something will be better. Something to represent my mood. Tonight, I need to go home and scrub all the parts where he touched me with antibacterial soap, and then I'm going to turn on my television to watch my old friend Ryuk.

On my way home my murderous impulses only increase. Okay, that's an exaggeration. I don't want to kill anyone, but I do want some of these people to fall in dog shit and scrape their knees or something.

I'm just trying to walk home from the bus stop, already stressed out from *Todd*, but I grit my teeth as I see these teenage morons standing on the corner of my block. They hang out there most days, always harass me, though I don't get why. I'm too old for them! I'm a grown ass woman and I'm not exactly a hot babe. I work hard to appear as bland as possible so I don't stand out, in fact. My clothes are plain and loose, my hair is in a simple bob, and I don't wear any makeup on my bespectacled face. But every time they're on the corner, which is most days, they catcall me and say gross stuff. It's so frustrating.

Today is the same as any other in that regard.

"Hey little mama, miss librarian with those glasses on, looking all smart and shit. Come here and give me a kiss," one of them hollers at me.

I grit my teeth and keep walking past. They never hurt me, just say stupid stuff. I'll just go past, get home, and relax with my television.

But today, things are different. Today they *touch me*.

"Hey, slow down sweetie, you don't got to look all mad. We just want to talk, you know?" A second one of them laughs and *grabs my arm*.

He steps up close to me and he smells like sour milk. I can see dried flecks of saliva on the corners of his pale lips, mysterious brown flecks in the stubble of his sparse, blonde mustache. *No, no, no.*

"DO NOT TOUCH ME!" I scream, pulling my arm away.

"Damn, crazy bitch," I hear behind me but I'm already running away to the middle of the block where my building is.

I unlock my apartment door and run up the stairs. As soon as I'm inside, I strip off my clothes and get in the shower, scrubbing my skin so hard it burns.

I fucking hate humans.

Chapter 4

Pillow

My Anne is not holding me in her delightfully passionate way tonight. As soon as she lay down on the bed to place her head on me, I could tell things were off. She smells like the strong soap, the one she uses when she's sad. She lays flat on her back, barely moving, only quietly observing those shows she likes. After hours of this she turns to her side, sniffles, and I feel a tear drop onto me.

If I had a heart it would break, seeing her like this. I want to hold her, to ask what's wrong, to help her, but I can't; I'm not strong enough yet. She's so sweet, so beautiful. She doesn't deserve any sort of suffering. She *needs* me, I know it. Insect energy barely keeps me firm and cool, it's not nearly enough to make myself *more*.

Oh, my Anne, my Anne, how can I help you?

A knock sounds from far outside the room. Anne sits up, holding me to her full chest, staying still, until another knock sounds. She sets me down and walks away.

Come back, please.

I immediately miss the warmth of her touch and I do not trust the knock at the door this late at night.

I hear voices coming from the other room, one of them hers, one of them male. If I could growl I would. Anne has never taken a mate since she's owned me, and I think I wouldn't be able to stand it if she did. She is *mine*.

"Yeah, you must have dropped it when you spilled your stuff like a silly goose. Thankfully your address is on your I.D. so I could bring it right over to you tonight. Would be a shame to not have your wallet if you needed it. Might even say you owe me a favor, right, Annie Banannie?" the male voice says.

"You could have given it to me tomorrow at work too, Todd. Thanks though. I'll see you later," Anne bites out.

She sounds much different than I've ever heard her. Granted, I usually only hear her when she's on the phone with her mother, playing online games with her internet friends, or making her sexy little noises when she uses me. But the way she sounds now is like none of those by far.

She sounds...upset.

"You know, I think I need to use the restroom. I'll just be a sec," the male voice says.

"That's not a good idea," Anne insists, but I hear

heavy footsteps start down the hall nonetheless, footsteps that do not belong to her.

"I'll just be a second. Oh, hey, is that your bedroom? Where the magic happens, am I right?" he, *Todd*, says.

His footsteps come even closer.

"Dude, get out. You said you had to pee, not wander my apartment. What the fuck?" My Anne raises her voice, and I can sense fear there.

This man is raising her alarms. Mine as well.

Then I see him. He enters her room and looks around, a lascivious grin on his pasty face as his eyes meet the bed. His disgusting cologne fills the room. I want to strangle him for covering the scent of my Anne for even a moment.

My Anne steps next to him, and he turns to face her, his grin only growing wider.

"Nice bed. I like your setup here with the T.V. and all. Why don't we sit here and watch a movie? Netflix and chill," he says with a creepy little laugh.

Todd sits down on the bed. My excitement builds.

Come a little closer. Just a *little* closer.

"Get out. This isn't funny," Anne cries.

She *cries*. This bastard is bringing tears to the eyes of my precious love. Now I'll feel no guilt at all when I do what I need to. *Not that I would anyway.*

"Oh, you're so silly, Annie. Come on, have a seat," he says.

He pats me to invite her over. *Yes.*

HE TOUCHES ME.

When his hand lands on me I suck the life out of him. It's much more difficult than with the bugs, I find. He struggles much harder. He tries to lift his hand but can't—I won't allow it.

"What the hell?" he forces out through choked breath.

If he's speaking, that means I'm not pulling hard enough. I yank on his life force, dragging it into me. I can see his skin dry out, become thinner, lose the glow of youth.

The power inside me grows. I'm strong. It feels *so good.*

"Todd? TODD!" Anne screams, wrenching him off of me.

He stands for barely a moment before collapsing to the ground. In the flash that I'm able to see him, I can tell he looks older, much older, though I didn't age him enough to kill him. *Oh well.* He *does* look old enough for death to come soon. Thin, gray hair, hollow cheeks, frail body, nearly skeletal...he won't be hurting my Anne any longer.

Anne looks around frantically, wiping her hands on

her pants as she searches for her phone. Seeing it finally, she grabs it, then drops it before picking it up with a growl of frustration. She sobs as she dials a three-digit number. I feel bad—for a moment; I don't want her to be upset but I know I did what had to be done. *It will be worth it, my love.*

"Please send an ambulance to 1775 Barkersville Lane. This guy collapsed I don't know what the fuck happened. Please hurry."

She talks some more for a few minutes on the phone, pacing up and down the hallway, occasionally peering down at Todd to make sure he's still breathing. Eventually some strangers arrive to take him away, and other strangers question Anne for a bit. It's late before they leave. She's so worn and tired that she doesn't even change into her pajamas before collapsing into bed with me.

She holds me as she sleeps, unaware that I'm doing something incredible inside of me. Something that will change both of us forever.

Tomorrow we'll be together. Anne, my Anne.

Chapter 5

Anne

Everyone stares at me all day at work. I can't freaking handle it, so I fake a migraine and leave early. They all know about what happened to Todd, somehow. I don't know how; I didn't tell them. Hell, I don't even really know what happened. One second he was on my bed being a creep and the next he was halfway to being a corpse. I didn't do anything to him, but I could tell by the way people looked at me that they certainly thought I did.

Why wouldn't they? I was the only one with him. *Whatever*, I'm going home and taking some me time away from their judgmental stares.

I stop by the market on the way home to grab my favorite brand of triangle-shaped corn chips and a bottle of peach Ramune soda. They're my comfort foods, and I could really use some comfort right now. I just want to go home, eat my snacks, sit in bed, and watch something I've seen a hundred times before. Nothing dark—I already feel gloomy as it is. I think I'll just find some magical girl show to keep me company.

As soon as I open the door to my apartment, I can sense something is off. There is a feeling in the air, this vibration, just something *wrong*. I know it's coming from my room. I have seen enough horror to know not to head toward what the weird thing is, but I can't help it. This is my apartment, and I can't just run away because there are some bad vibes, right?

It's probably just me being paranoid because of last night. I shake my head and walk toward my room instead of the kitchen like I'd planned, needing to prove to myself right away that I'm just being a scaredy cat.

When I get to my room, my hand clenches in surprise, causing my bag of chips to burst, making a loud *pop* sound. The smell of nacho cheese wafts upward. I drop the soda bottle from my right hand, shattering the glass. Sweet, carbonated beverage sprays all over my feet, all over the walls, and in the direction of my bed.

My bed, where some horrible thing is pulsing and stretching.

What the fuck is it?

Chapter 6

Pillow

My Anne stands in the doorway in shock. I understand why she's upset; I'm not fully formed. She isn't supposed to be home for hours and I haven't finished building myself yet. *Damn.*

As of right now my lower half is mostly formed. I have feet, legs, hips, even pants. None of it is fully detailed, but it's started at least. My upper half, however, is a mess.

My chest, arms, and head are simply four pillows. They aren't even particularly firm or attractive pillows at the moment, they're only blank placeholders for upcoming pieces. It's quite embarrassing to be seen this way after spending so many years making myself into the perfect pillow, I must say.

Not all of my upper half is blank though. Part of a face is formed on the topmost pillow—a dent of a mouth and eyes only, but that's it. The eyes are well formed, sitting in the center of the topmost pillow, turning toward Anne to watch her as her face drains of color.

Oh, dear. I can imagine having fully formed eyes rolling around in all that white space probably looks quite gruesome. *Damn, again.*

All the rest of me is soft, feather-filled cotton that is bubbling, growing, and stretching—the process which will make me into a fully formed man. But for now, that form is more of a…pillow sludge.

All of that is to say, I look like a goddamn monster.

I open what I have of a mouth to try to speak. Out comes something that doesn't help me seem any less monstrous. My "voice" sounds as if a creaking door and an old air conditioner had a child and shat it into my mouth. Anne begins to hyperventilate. I begin to panic. What do I do now?

Alright, I'll focus on building my communication skills.

I put all of my effort into all the parts of me most responsible for speech, until I can at least make a sound that won't send her into cardiac arrest—I think. She looks like she's going to faint by the time I'm done, even though it doesn't take me long, so I try to choose my words carefully.

"Anne," I rasp out. My voice isn't perfect yet but it's not horrible. It's whispery and rough but it's getting better. "Don't be afraid, please. I won't harm you. Please forgive me for my appearance, I shall fix it shortly."

Anne blinks once, twice then to my relief, speaks to me. "Oh. Okay then."

I smile as much as I can with a mouth that's hardly more than two folds in fabric. She accepts me.

My Anne, of course, would accept me. She's meant for me. My Anne is...

...on the floor. She fainted. *Damn*.

Alright, time to make a functioning body so I can help her. I'll worry about appearance later I suppose, though I hope I don't scare her again.

Why did she have to come home early? Of all the days.

I focus on working arms and legs, everything I need to walk and lift my Anne. I'm panicking by the time I get to her, knowing I still look hideous, but I do get to her, nonetheless. I lift her carefully and take her to the bed where I lay her down on one of her inferior pillows. I don't really know what else to do other than wait; I'm only a pillow after all. I don't exactly have emergency medical education. So, I just sit next to her and continue building myself.

Anne is out for a long time. I am able to finish my shape, however my details are not completed when she wakes. My hair is just a vague blob and I have little color to speak of. I have, however, been able to add some shading to my facial features with the ink that was on my tag, so I do look more human and less monster. Yes, I look like a sketch, a drawing, but a drawing of a human at least.

Anne opens her eyes and looks at my newly built face. I smile again, this time with a mouth that's more than just a few dents in woven cotton.

"Hello again," I say in a much clearer voice than before. "Welcome back."

Chapter 7

Anne

I open my eyes and see before me a living animation. Or something. What the hell is it? Is that the thing from before? I slide away from whatever it is, until I am at the opposite edge of the bed.

"What are you?" I stammer out.

My body shakes. I feel like I should run but there's nowhere to go. If I wanted to leave the room I would have to go past the...thing, so it's pointless. *Fuck.*

"Well, that's complicated," it says, smiling with a mouth that looks as if it were drawn with ink. "The simplest answer, I suppose, would be that I am your pillow. Your favorite pillow. I've just changed a bit, as you can see."

"No shit." One quick, hysterical bubble of laughter escapes me before going silent again. "What are you doing here?"

"I...upgraded myself today. I'm not complete. Building a person takes a lot of detailed work, but I'm getting closer. I am saving the fine details until I get your input. You see, I built myself for *you*, Anne.

You should decide on my final form."

I'm silent for a while before replying slowly and carefully, "What do you mean 'built myself for you'?"

"Anne, I have been in love with you for years. I have kept myself firm and cool for you and tried every day to find a way to become *more*. Today I have done it. We can finally be together. You are my love; make me yours."

"Okay well that's pretty intense. And look dude, I'm not even sure I'm not hallucinating," I say as I rub my temples.

Either I'm going insane, or I have some kind of pillow monster who is moving way too fast in the relationship department in my bedroom. Neither of those situations seem appealing.

"I assure you I'm real. I'm too aware that I'm inhuman and appear to be as such, quite so, but I am working on changing that. Just give me a short while, please. It will be much easier to accept the reality of the situation when I don't appear so... strange."

He looks embarrassed and I actually feel kind of bad for him. I can't imagine being in his situation.

"So, uh, what can I do to help?" I ask. I cross my arms over my ample chest nervously, not really sure what else to do.

He perks up, sitting straight, his face seeming to

light up as much as cotton and ink can. "Please, just tell me what your ideal man would be. I want to be everything you desire. My only reason for being is to please you, Anne. Help me."

"So, that's a lot," I begin, standing up and moving away from the bed. "I hope you understand that I don't exactly like people."

"I know, Anne, I know you. That's why you must understand that I'm not like them. I'm not flesh and blood. When you touch me there will be no sweat, no germs, nothing to fear. I'll only appear how you want me to. I'll only touch you how you want me to. I'll never make you sick. never betray you or insult you. I'll never hurt you. I'm yours, Anne. Please, complete me."

My mind races as I think of all the possibilities. I could have everything I've ever wanted. But this... this is *wrong*. Isn't it? It can't be right to mess with the universe like this. And yet, I want the ability to *touch*. But I've wanted only animated guys—yet here is someone with *a drawing for a face* telling me he'll be anything I want him to be.

I nibble on my thumbnail, trying to prevent myself from messing with my fingertips. They've gotten dry as hell from all the stress rubbing lately and it's distracting. I need to think right now. If I could finally have the ability to touch someone, maybe even a boyfriend type someone, shouldn't I take it? And if I could create him to look however I want what would I do? *This is tough.* I lower my hand and nod as I make my decision.

"Well, there's this anime butler," I say. "I think that's a good place to start if we're working on appearance."

Chapter 8

Pillow

My Anne and I work for hours to get my form correct. She requests that I be tall and lean, my brows arched, handsome in a nearly androgynous way. I'm provided with the markers she uses for sketching design ideas to absorb colors for my pale flesh. Of course, I'm easily able to create the perfect designs for my elegant clothing; I'm made of fabrics after all.

When I'm done I'm precisely as she requested. My dark hair falls over one eye. I bite a pouty lip seductively as I watch her inspect me one final time for anything she may have missed. She's so, so beautiful and now that I'm complete I hope…I hope she'll accept me.

"Wow, you look great," she exclaims.

I exhale powerfully, relieved beyond measure to hear those words.

"Obviously if anyone got too close they'd see you're made of fabric. I mean, I think the being made of fabric thing is awesome, but you'll just have to not get super close to other people I guess."

"That's not a problem. I don't care about anyone else, only you."

"Man, you're really killing me. You seriously only exist because of me?" She crosses her arms over her chest again in that way that means she's nervous.

I don't want her to feel anxious around me but I can't help coming across a bit...intense. Being aware but unable to move, communicate, or even let anyone know I was sentient for years may have had a small effect on my sanity. Or at the very least my ability to properly tone down my feelings for the comfort of others.

"Oh, Anne. You have no idea how much you mean to me. You are the reason I exist and the reason I want to keep existing."

"Well, I feel kind of weird. I mean, how long have you been sentient? Because I've, uh, done stuff..." Her face turns bright red, and she holds herself even tighter than before.

I can only assume *stuff* means her wonderful *grinding* sessions.

"I've been sentient for quite a while now. If you're wondering whether I've been aware when you've ground your gorgeous cunt against me the answer is *yes.*"

Anne takes a sharp breath and covers her face with

her hands.

"Oh my god," she whispers from behind those small hands. "I'm so embarrassed."

"Don't be. It was beautiful. You brought me to life, Anne. I hope one day to experience that again, to have you grind against my face, as I thrust my tongue into your wet center, and rub your throbbing clit. You wouldn't have to do it all yourself anymore, my darling. I'm here to serve you."

I take a risk and slowly, tentatively, step toward her. Watch her reaction so, so carefully to make sure she doesn't panic. I raise my brand-new hand to caress her rosy cheek. She doesn't pull away. My heart races.

She doesn't pull away.

"Anne, let me serve you." I run my fingers through her brown hair and her eyes close. "Come with me."

I step back and hold out my hand. The decision is now hers. My feather heart pounds as I wait for her to decide.

Please, please, take my hand.

"I should be afraid but you're...irresistible. What is it about you?" she asks as she takes my hand.

Yes, my heart rejoices as she takes my hand. How do I answer her?

Because we're meant to be together. Because I am

literally made for you. Because I will do anything it takes to claim you, serve you, and keep you.

No, I know what she would like to hear. I grin as I reply in a partial quote I know she'll love.

"I'm simply one hell of a pillow."

Chapter 9

Anne

I take his hand and a sharp breath; the feeling is so strange, though not uncomfortable by any means. Normally I would be flinching away in disgust at any touch, but this is different. He's not flesh, he's not greasy and sweaty. When I touch him it's just cool, firm, fabric. I sigh in relief and let him lead me to the bed where we sit on the edge next to one another. He sets our hands on my knee, his on top of mine and smiles at me silently.

"What now?" I ask with a soft, nervous laugh.

"Whatever you'd like. You have a man who would do anything for you, a man you've built to your specifications, who can't make you sick, who'll never hurt you. What would you like to do with me?" He speaks in a raspy voice right against my neck, sounding as if his every muscle is tense with anticipation.

"Whatever I'd like? What if I just want to do stuff that isn't super...sexual?" My face heats when I say it, but I don't know how else to phrase it. "I mean, I just met you."

"Well, you haven't just met me; I've been here for years. I understand what you mean though," he says with a soft laugh. "I said we can do whatever you want, and I mean it.

"Just because I came off strong doesn't mean you have to do what I spoke of. I only know what I've been taught by you, I should let you know that. Everything I know about the world came from what you've said to visitors, on your phone, what you've watched on your screens, et cetera. I admit I have a fondness for the hentai you watch and perhaps that influenced my initial enthusiasm."

He smirks as my cheeks heat.

"But I know how much you love so many other things, and I love them too because of that. I will be your partner in all things. Just tell me."

"You've watched the hentai? Oh no. Oh no, no, no. Even the stuff with the tentacles?" I cover my face with my hands and lean forward.

"Oh yes. I have a special fondness for that, actually. I've seen everything you've watched here, Anne, and I've been here every time you've touched yourself to it. Think of how many times you've ground yourself against me until you came. Don't be embarrassed; you've made me so, so happy."

I flop backwards onto the bed and stare at the ceiling. I have one of those ugly lights that looks like a boob, the kind you find in like every apartment. The landlord keeps saying they're going to replace it with new more energy efficient lights, but they also said they were going to replace the air conditioner, and it's eighty degrees in here, so yeah, right. Why am I focusing on the light?

I turn back toward the pillow and my breath catches as I really, fully take in how gorgeous he is. As I was working to design him it was like a puzzle and though I paid attention to the pieces, now that I am looking at the completed man, he's...wow. Every dreamboat in my favorite anime–or anything else real or fiction–has nothing on him. I might literally swoon.

"Maybe we can, um, hold hands for a little while?" I manage to squeak out.

He grins with a perfectly white smile. "Of course. Come here, we'll lay on these inferior pillows."

We climb up onto the bed next to one another, sitting propped up on my pillows, and I hold his hand. I feel silly but considering I haven't willingly touched another person in years, this is a pretty big deal. I clear my throat and decide to make conversation.

"Do you have a name? I mean, I can't call you 'Pillow' forever."

"I do not. Perhaps you'll give me one? I would like that a lot." He smiles at me, and I notice he has a dimple.

I didn't suggest the dimple but it's perfect.

"That's a pretty big responsibility, but I guess someone has to give you a name and I'm the only person you know. Let's see."

I look him over and take in all of his features: dark hair, bright eyes, pale skin, long and lean body, soft and full lips, elegant hands, broad shoulders, big feet. I realize as I'm looking that I didn't build his... uh, *disco stick*. He created his pants before I paid attention to that part. I wonder if I'll be in charge of that or if he'll do it.

"Anne?" He interrupts my thoughts and I realize I have been thinking for a long time.

Oops, caught thinking about dick.

"Sorry, just thinking hard. What about Ori? It's an actual name, a really pretty name, and it kind of sounds a little bit like 'pillow' in French, if you mangle the word a lot. I think. I haven't taken French since high school. That's fun, right? Or is it dumb? It's pretty either way though, I think."

"I love it. *Ori*. I am now a man with a name. Who would have thought only hours ago I was simply a place to rest your head? You can still do that, of course, but now we can do lots of other fun things." He smiles again, showing that adorable dimple and squeezes my hand.

"Yep, you can order Starbucks now that you have a name for them to put on your cup. Very cool." I nod my head with a faux serious expression on my face.

"Oh, yes, of course. That is exactly the sort of thing I had in mind." When he laughs at my little joke it's deep and throaty.

It's the kind of laugh the hero in a story has, the one that swoops the love interest away at the last minute when she gets nearly overwhelmed in battle; the one she nearly kisses episode after episode but never quite does until the very last season and when she does it's absolute fireworks. I squirm in my spot at the sound of it. *Is anything about him not perfect*?

Ori sits up, faces me, and reaches out to stroke my cheek. "Anne, I—"

His head flops forward, his neck bent over in an entirely flat seam. A wheezing, burbling sound releases briefly before there is only silence. His head wobbles flat against his chest.

"Ori!" I panic, pushing him down to the bed.

He looks normal, except there is a crease in the fabric of the center of his neck, cutting off his breathing.

His eyes swivel to my face. He grimaces. His hands push against his chest under where I am bent over him. I move away to watch what's happening. Slowly he pushes whatever fills the volume inside of him—feathers if he's still mostly pillow—into his neck, filling it back up again. He lets out a gasp and sits up, wrapping his arms around me, holding tight.

"Ori, what the hell happened?" I squeak out.

"I think I need a little more power. Being both pillow and man is fine, good for *us* even, but I think I might be weighted a little too heavily on the pillow side currently. I'm afraid if I don't get a bit more power I might fall apart." He takes a shuddering breath. "I'm a little frightened, Anne."

"Ori," I say as I unwrap his arms from around me. I put my hands on either side of his face and look him square in the eyes. "Tell me what we have to do to keep you safe."

Chapter 10

Ori

Oh dear. I don't want her to reject me, but I do need her help. I knew this could be a problem, only hoped it wouldn't be. I really don't want her to think I'm a monster but if I want to be more solid I have no choice.

Here goes nothing, as they say.

"Anne, to get my life I need to take bits from others. I was—I know this may be disturbing but forgive me —I was surviving on the life energy of *insects* until recently."

"Oh, that explains all the dead flies and stuff I find in my bed sometimes."

"Yes, my apologies." I grimace before continuing. "It wasn't enough to build myself into more than the rectangle I was, however, so I needed something larger. When that man came over, that disgusting *Todd*, I may have sipped from him a bit."

I rub the back of my neck and shrug my shoulders.

Anne sits silently for a moment before barking out a

laugh. "That's what happened to that creep? He got drained by a vampire pillow? I mean, I should feel like scared of you, or bad for Todd, or something but he's a massive asshole. I have no doubt he was going to try something *really bad* with me that night so like...good job."

She holds up her hand for a high five and I give her one, breathing out a sigh of relief. There is more to tell her but at least that part is covered. Now, onto the next.

"I'm glad you're not upset. I am continuing to have a problem with my body, however. I am not quite man enough, yet—too much pillow. I'm going to continue to have these..." I point to where my neck was flopping earlier, "...episodes if I don't get a bit stronger."

"Okay, so how do we do it then? I don't think we can get Todd back over here," she says with a snort.

"No, I don't believe so. I don't suppose you know any other 'massive assholes' you wouldn't mind being drained of their life forces?"

I laugh until I notice she isn't laughing. *Oh dear.*

"I wasn't serious, please don't be upset."

"No, it's okay. I think I do know other creeps. A lot of them. You can just take a little at a time though, right? It doesn't have to be a whole bunch like with Todd?"

"Yes. I can take *very* small amounts. I believe I can, at least, I haven't tried it on a person but the amounts I take from insects are so small I am assuming I can take the same from people."

My Anne grins in a way that reminds me of a certain classic, animated, green Christmas creature looking to steal presents. She rubs her hands together and *cackles*.

"Let's go for a walk."

Chapter 11

Anne

I'm not a cruel person, I swear, I just really don't like people who grab onto me without permission. The idea of having a tiny bit of revenge is too delicious to resist. Grabbing my purse and Ori's hand on the way, I grin like a fiend as I march toward the front door.

"Where are we going, my love?" he asks so sweetly.

"You won't *really* hurt anyone, right? And you can take the life force, or whatever it's called, fast?" I ask as I shut the door behind us and start down the street. "So, let's say you just brush up against someone. You could take a little bit, right? You only need a little more mojo, meaning you'd only need a few people, so if we just took from a handful of jerks it wouldn't be too bad of a thing."

"Yes to all of that but what are you planning, Anne?"

"Follow me."

Ori follows my commands blindly and for a moment I feel a little guilty, like I'm bossing him around, until he stumbles next to me. I nearly tumble down with him when he dips downward. When I look in the direction I'm falling, I see that his thigh has bent flat in half.

"One moment please," he pleads, falling to one knee as he adjusts his stuffing to refill his thigh. Once he's finished he stands up and retakes my hand. "My apologies. Let us continue."

I don't feel so bad pulling him along now. He needs this, he needs me to take him to these guys. Ori is a sweetheart and I can't let him fall apart just because I'm too chicken to be a little bit ruthless. The thought of him getting hurt—or worse—because of my hesitation frightens me more than I thought it would.

So, I take him to the corner where the teenage jerks hang out and sure enough they're there. A little before we get to the corner I drag Ori over to the shadow of a building where I can talk to him a little more privately. My fingertips itch to be soothed but I grab Ori's hands instead.

"See those guys? They called me names and grabbed my arm and stuff. They're really young, like nineteen years old I think, so if you take just a tiny bit they won't miss it. They're huge jerks and they deserve it anyway. Okay?"

My stomach kind of hurts when I say it. I mean, it's definitely not like I'm Light Yagami or something, I'm not killing them, but it's not a nice thing to do.

A flapping sound distracts me. I see Ori's ear blowing

wildly in the breeze, nothing more now than flat fabric against his head as he smiles his adorably dimpled smile and tells me, "Of course. I would do anything for you, my Anne."

No, it's not a nice thing to do but for Ori it's the *right* thing to do.

Chapter 12

Ori

Anne and I walk to the corner of her street where some hooligans are crowded near a bus stop. The ruffians begin shouting as soon as they see her.

"Hey look, that crazy girl has a man."

"Girl, when'd you get a man? How about a real man, huh?"

My anger flares hot inside me. Oh, I'm going to enjoy taking life from them, even though it won't be much.

Anne is silent as we walk through their group, silent even as they *touch her face.* Yes, one taps on her cheek as we walk past, and if she would have allowed it, I would have done whatever I could to have torn that man's arm right off. *No one touches my Anne but me.* But no, she wouldn't want that. Instead of indulging my more violent fantasies, I subtly drag my fingers across their exposed hands and arms, incredibly lightly, as we walk past, enjoying the shivers and brief flare of dullness in each of their eyes as I touch them.

By the time we pass they're all silent, confused looks on their faces. We turn the corner and head around the block, back to her apartment, unspeaking the entire way.

When we get inside she stomps to the bathroom, slamming the door shut. I hear the water running and I know she must be washing the touch from her face.

The memory of his dry, cracked fingers on her soft, freckled skin makes my stomach feel like it's filled with lead and my fists clench. If I could return I would take more life from them. *Bastards*. But no, I will always do what Anne desires and she told me only to take a little, so now the only thing I take are deep breaths until I'm calm. I work on making myself more solid.

When Anne returns I am built up much more strongly than I was before. There should be no falling apart now. There's only one bit of me left to create and I've saved some energy for that. It's important I have her input on that part more than any other, however, so I'll wait until she's ready to help me.

"How are you feeling, Ori?" she asks as she walks into the bedroom, drying her face, now red from scrubbing, and sets her glasses on the small table next to her bed.

"Wonderful. Our mission was a success." I raise my

arms and do a slow spin with a wide grin on my face, showing her that I am whole and solid.

"That's fantastic, because I want to take you up on your earlier offer." Anne tosses the towel into her laundry basket and shakes her damp hair out.

"What do you mean?" My heart rate increases; she can't mean what I think she means.

My darling Anne wraps her arms around my neck, gazing up into my wide eyes. "It's time I finally experienced real touch, Ori, and I can't think of anyone better to try it with than you. I know I've just found you but you're perfect. When I thought you were hurt...I was scared, Ori. Even though I didn't know you, I wanted to help you so much. I would have been devastated to lose you. It's weird to feel like that so soon but I don't care, this whole thing is fucking weird as hell, right? So, let's go for it. Touch me, Ori."

My hands slightly shake as I tuck her hair behind her ears, run my fingertips along her jaw, my thumb across her barely parted lips.

"Do you want more touch than this?" I pause with my palm against her cheek.

Anne is breathing hard, her eyes closed. Her little pink tongue darts across her lips before she opens those bright eyes and looks into mine.

"Please. Touch me everywhere, Ori."

"Gladly."

Using my new strength, I grab my love under her thick rump and lift her until she is face to face with me. Her arms wrap around my neck and her legs wrap around my waist, pushing her body flush against me. I barely hold back a moan at the feeling. I take a breath of time to memorize this moment before I walk her to the bed, laying her down flat on her back. Her hair spreads around her face, chest heaving, and her legs remain spread wide around my hips as I loom over her. I've never had this view of her. *She's perfect.*

"Is this too weird? To move this fast?" Anne's adorable, freckled nose scrunches up in concern. "It's just, I mean, you're so hot and nice and I'm really excited to experience all the things I never have before, you know? But if you think this is bad then we can slow it down, okay?"

The hem of Anne's t-shirt slides smoothly over her stomach as I drag it slowly up her body.

"Why wait? We know what we want." I slip the shirt the rest of the way over her head and *tsk* when she crosses her arms over her chest.

"None of that now, I want to see all of you," I admonish her as I move her arms to her sides and reach behind her to unclasp her bra.

It's a bit harder with my inexperienced fingers than

I expected but after a few giggles on both our ends I manage to get it undone. Anne lets out a shaky breath as I pull the bra from her body, revealing her full chest to me.

I can feel my new pupils expand as I gaze down at her lovely breasts. The large mounds of them fall heavily to the side as she's lying flat on her back. Her nipples are hard already, and the area around them is a soft pinkish brown. I can't resist dragging the pad of my thumb over one of those peaked nipples, making her arch up into my hand with a soft hiss.

"Your skin…it doesn't feel exactly like skin. I mean, it feels like how a thumb should be sort of rough, but it also feels like…well, fabric." Anne takes my hand and inspects it. "It looks much more like flesh than it did before we left the house earlier, and it does feel like it at first, but on my lips and, um, nipple I could tell it wasn't. On my sensitive spots, basically, it felt more like denim than skin."

"Did that upset you?" I roll off of her and lie next to her. *Have I disgusted her?*

"Oh no, not at all." She rolls over to face me, grabbing my face in her hands. "It's perfect. I freaking love it. Seriously. If this trend continues and I don't have to worry about you feeling like skin in my other sensitive spots then I am going to be ecstatic, Ori, for real. In fact, we should check right now to see if it's just your thumbs that feel like fabric."

Anne blinks her eyes slowly, moves her face closer to mine, pulling me toward her. *Yes.* Our lips part slightly, and we meet in a soft kiss. After several quick, gentle kisses, she slips her tongue into my mouth, seeking mine. I'm only too happy to greet her. She moans as our tongues tangle together, and she presses her unclothed chest against my shirt.

Pulling away finally she takes a ragged breath, brushing away the hair that has fallen into my eyes.

"Satin. Your mouth feels like the slipperiest, smoothest satin." She rests her head on my chest and lets out a breathless laugh. "It's too perfect. This has to be a dream."

I pet her hair and pull her tight against me. "Not a dream, my darling Anne, though I admit I question the reality of it myself every time you allow me the blessing of your touch."

Anne groans and pushes away from me. "You're too freaking sweet, I can't stand it."

She fusses with a button on my shirt, pouting. "Why am I topless and you're still fully dressed? Take off your clothes, right now."

"Gladly, dear."

As I begin to unbutton my shirt, Anne leans over and begins to kiss me, her hands running through my hair. I fumble through the work of unbuttoning, distracted by her perfect tongue, somehow managing after an awkwardly long moment. I work my arms out of the sleeves, pulling away from the kiss as I turn to toss the shirt onto the floor.

"I'll pick it up later, I promise." I laugh.

When I turn back to Anne, she isn't laughing one bit. She's staring at my exposed torso, her mouth slightly ajar, eyes wide. Anne reaches out her small hand and runs her fingers from my neck to the waistband of my pants.

"Damn, we really did a good job designing you didn't we? I mean, you looked good before but after you got that extra juice from those corner guys you really... wow."

I look down at my body to see what she's talking about and notice that I have become more defined. I look quite fantastic indeed. Smirking, I lie back on my elbows.

"I wonder if the rest of me looks as good, hmm?" When she goes to hastily grab the button on my pants, I stop her hand. "You first."

"Rude!" she scoffs, feigning outrage, but I can see the glint of playfulness in her eyes. "Fine."

She tugs her jeans off with no gracefulness, sticking her tongue out at me, making me laugh. When she's left in nothing but her blue, cotton underwear she grabs the button on my pants once again.

"Now it's you, dang it."

Still laughing, I let her undo my button, unzip my zipper, and slowly tug my pants from my hips. My laughter dies out when she straddles my thighs and runs her fingers along the waistband of my black undergarments. I'm forced to stop her hands once again, this time with a sigh.

"We have to talk."

Chapter 13

Anne

"What's wrong?" I cock my head to the side, confused. I thought he'd want me to get into his pants. I mean, I noticed it's pretty, uh, flat in his underwear but I'm thinking maybe he's just nervous. Or maybe his parts are super small? Either way, I don't care, I want him to feel comfortable as much as I want to touch him.

Jeez that feels weird, wanting to touch someone. For the first time, though, I feel that desire.

"Nothing is wrong, my love, we simply need to finish something. You see, we still need to complete my cock." Ori blushes as he says that final word, then clears his throat. "And the rest of the bits too, I suppose."

"Ooh! Okay! So, I get to like decide what it's going to look like and stuff?" I raise an eyebrow.

"Exactly. You'll be the only one who gets to benefit from it so why shouldn't you get to decide its features? Just like the rest of me, it belongs to you, Anne."

I wiggle my fingers in front of me in a steeple formation. "Mwa, ha, ha. This is going to be fun."

I pause for a moment to think of what I should do until a thought occurs to me.

"Wait, I have no idea what I want, realistically." Flopping down next to Ori on the bed, I pout at my realization. "I thought I was going to be a sexy Doctor Frankenstein there for a second, but I don't know anything about sex that isn't from hentai or like movies."

We sit in thoughtful silence until Ori breaks it.

"We could start with what you do know, perhaps? We've seen them on the internet when you've browsed your laptop lying in bed. You only need to give me a vague idea of which one you'd like to start with. Then we can adjust from there."

"That's a good idea. I grew up on the internet, I've seen dicks before. I always quickly looked away because...ugh, people, but still. Okay. Maybe, uh, well there was that one picture that was kind of nice that I even paused on recently before deleting it that those trolls posted under my comment on the Visual Novels Creators Forum. It was like, I don't know, six inches and a little thick and it didn't curve much or anything, I guess. Can you try that?"

I put my hands on my cheeks, feeling how hot they are. *Ugh this is awkward.*

"Right away, my dear," Ori replies with a dashing grin.

Soon enough a bulge begins to inflate in his underpants. I stifle a giggle at the sight. It's less like a cock growing hard and more like a balloon inflating. It's just so silly, but when it's finally done the outline of it is definitely *not* a balloon. My mouth goes dry at the sight of it. My fingers itch to pull down that waistband—*finally*.

"Ori, is it time for me to look?" I manage to choke out.

"I believe so, yes. Remember I can change anything."

I slide my fingers under the waistband of his black undergarments and slip them slowly down. His freshly created cock springs free, and I gasp. It's exactly as I asked for, beautiful if ever one could be described as such, and balls to match.

"Is it alright then?" he asks, his voice barely above a whisper.

I look up to see his cheeks have turned shockingly pink.

"Are you feeling shy?"

My eyebrows practically raise to the ceiling. So far I've been the super awkward one but right now he looks nervous as heck. I can't resist poking at him a little bit; he's just too cute.

"No…I mean, a bit, yes." He crosses his arms over his chest, uncrosses them, then crosses them again, seeming as if he no longer has any idea what to do with his body.

"Well, you don't have to be nervous. You look super-hot."

Ori exhales sharply, tense muscles relaxing.

"However," I continue, and he inhales deeply again, eyes wide, "I think I should sample the goods before deciding if they're satisfactory, shouldn't I?"

I toss a leg over his so that his lovely cock juts up before me. I can see his chest rise and fall quickly as the speed of his breathing increases.

"That sounds like the correct choice, I believe. Only rational, yes," he chokes out.

I lick my finger and run the tip of it down the length of him, watching his face as he makes a strangled noise. I can't help but giggle at his reaction. If just that small touch made him react that way then what will even more bring?

This time I bend over, take him into my hand, and run my tongue up his shaft and around the top of him. Ori sits up so fast he nearly smashes his face into mine. He puts his hands on either side of my face and kisses the top of my head, my cheek, my shoulder.

"Sorry," he says as he lays back down. "Brand new

equipment and all. It needs a bit of calibration I think. By which I mean I need a moment or two before I receive the focus of your attention or I'll just make a mess everywhere."

Ori runs a long-fingered hand through his increasingly messy mop of dark hair.

"Besides, I want to focus on your pleasure, Anne. I want to please you, to make love to you."

I lay my head on his chest and consider the next steps between us. This is all very fast but very exciting. His cock is pressed against my stomach. Feeling how hard and thick it is gets me a bit nervous about the whole sex thing.

"So, we can adjust as we go, right? I just want to make sure we're on the same page," I ask as I sit up, looking him in the eye.

If we're going to have fun I want to make sure I don't offend him by doing the build-a-dick thing during it.

"You absolutely will not offend me if that's what you're concerned about. I want you to make me perfect, tell me what you desire, my darling."

"This might be weird but what if we adjust it while it's, uh, inside me? I mean, we could find the perfect size if it's literally inside, right? Is that dumb?" I rub my fingers together nervously, waiting for his reactions.

"That's not in any way a foolish suggestion. In fact, I

think it's brilliant. Who else in the world would have that opportunity?" He sits up and strokes the side of my cheek, eyelids heavy with desire. "Shall we give it a go then?"

Chapter 14

Ori

"Um, I'll be right back." Anne jumps off the bed and sprints to the bathroom, shutting the door behind her.

Hmm. Well, she's either too nervous or needs a moment to clean up, I'm assuming. Then again, I know very little about women so who knows really? I lie back with an arm behind my head and wait for her to return.

It only takes a bit for her to come back to me. I watch only too gladly as she walks back down the hall toward me in her little cotton panties, her full breasts bouncing, her cheeks red with a shy blush.

"Come to me, my love, and lay next to me." I slide over and pat the bed beside me, and she follows my instruction. "Take off your panties and spread your legs for me, let me see your pretty cunt."

I decide to be forward with her, with it being her first time and all. She's likely to be a bit nervous and in need of direction. I admit I'm a nervous virgin as well but, being a pillow, I don't have the virginity hang ups people do and so I feel it's my responsibility to take the lead.

Her breath comes out as shaky as her hands as she slowly removes her panties. She looks away shyly as she opens her legs for me, not saying a word. I climb between them, on my knees before her.

"You're magnificent, Anne. Spread your lips for me, I want to see all of you."

She makes a squeaking sound. "Ori!" she yelps before attempting to close her legs, but she can't when I'm between them.

"*Tsk*. Don't deny me now, please. Be a naughty girl for once, my sweet Anne." My lip curls on one side when she takes a sharp breath and opens wide again.

She places one hand on her breast and the other cups the dark curls on her enticing mound. She uses two fingers to spread the outer lips of her folds, showing me the inside of her offerings. I groan as I crawl forward, needing to witness that pink perfection as close as possible.

"Anne," I beg in a voice so strained I can barely scratch it out, "may I taste you?"

"Oh. Yes, please. That would be great actually." She giggles. I grin at the sound.

Inhaling her scent as I kiss my way up her inner thigh, the clean, light, fragrance goes straight to my newly formed cock. My eyes meet hers, seeking assurance one last time, and she gives a tiny nod. It's all I need before I playfully swat her hand away from her glistening cunt and plant my face there instead.

My satin tongue glides through her slippery folds, pushing deep into her core, teasing her, then out again to circle the firm bud of her clitoris. She pulls my head against her sweet heat and grinds against my face, using me roughly as if I were simply the pillow of before, only now I've got lips and tongue and teeth to further the pleasure.

She pulls me harder against her, so hard that a normal man wouldn't be able to breathe. Thankfully, being mostly a pillow I can last much longer without air and can survive her overpowering embrace until I feel her shake and tense around me. Wetness floods against me as she cries out in pleasure. *Yes.* This is what I've dreamed of for so long.

"Ori, oh fuck, that was amazing. I can't believe it." Anne pants when her climax is complete. She pulls me up by the ears to meet her eye-to-eye and when her barely focused eyes take in my face finally she yelps and pushes me away. "Your face!"

"What is it?" I look into the mirror on the closet door only to see I've been flattened a bit, mostly my nose. *Oh my.* "Oh, well, it appears I only need to fluff myself back up. Apologies."

I give myself a few pats and like a good pillow I am

back in tip top shape.

"Okay. I keep forgetting you're a pillow. Huh. I suppose I was grinding kind of hard." Anne snorts out a laugh.

"Not that I minded one bit." I slide a finger along the seam of her pussy, feeling how incredibly wet she is, and making her hiss in surprise. "And you certainly enjoyed it. That's all that matters to me."

"I really did enjoy it. Very much, thank you." Anne bites her lip. "I think I'm ready to, you know."

"To what, Anne?" I fit myself between her thighs when she doesn't answer me, one of my hands goes to her hair as the other lazily strokes a nipple. "Tell me, you have to say it. You're ready to what?"

"You know what I want, Ori." Anne runs her fingers through my sleek, dark hair.

I put my mouth against her ear, run my tongue along that lovely shell until she moans.

"Say it," I demand. "I need to hear it. Do you want me to fuck you, my sweet? Do you want my cock inside you, the one you've created to be perfect just for you? I've spent years thinking of being inside your hot, wet, cunt and I need to hear you tell me I'm allowed to be there. My entire existence is for you, I want nothing more than your pleasure in all things, and I promise them to you, if only you'll allow it. So, say it, my darling. Say the words."

"Yes, please. Fuck me, Ori, now, I need it." Anne grips my hips and pushes me against her wet center.

I grin against the crook of her neck in relief.

"As you wish."

Chapter 15

Anne

I'm begging for a pillow to fuck me. What kind of day is this? I mean, he's in man form but still. This has to be the first time in history it's ever happened. I'm seriously about to lose my virginity to a *living pillow*. Holy shit.

You know, this is kind of...awesome, actually. I'm not going to complain.

Ori runs a finger between my folds, making me sigh in delight, but when he inserts two fingers slowly into my pussy I find myself making a desperate, keening noise I've never made before.

"Is this alright?" Ori asks, sounding almost breathless as he carefully plunges his fingers in and out of me.

"Yes," I mewl. "It feels good."

"Are you ready for me then, my love?"

"Yes, I am." I look into his eyes and nod, reassuring him.

He smiles softly, showing that dimple I like so much.

Ori adjusts my hips slightly before aligning the tip of his cock against my center. I can see his throat bob right before he begins to enter me, and I have a brief moment to realize he might be even more anxious than I am, considering how long he's waited for this. It's only a moment of thought, because next thing I know, I feel him pushing inside.

He moves agonizingly slowly. I'm super wet and turned on, so it goes pretty easy at first, but after a bit it starts to hurt just a little.

"Wait, stop." I put my hands on his shoulders. "Be, uh, smaller for a second. You're kind of big I guess, and it hurts a little. Maybe we can get it in smaller and then see about going bigger?"

Ori chuckles softly. "Brilliant idea."

He shrinks inside me; it's a strange sort of relief.

"Is this alright?"

"Much better. Now kiss me," I plead.

Ori obliges by giving me the hottest, deepest kiss imaginable. I groan into his mouth at the fantastic feeling and when he starts moving into me again it's the perfect slippery compliment to his tongue.

"That feels so fucking good." My voice is so much higher than normal when he breaks the kiss to lick and suck my neck as he slips in and out of me in a slow, smooth rhythm.

"*You* feel so good," I add. "Your cock is like some impossible combination of velvet, silk, and latex. So soft and smooth, feels like nothing I could have imagined."

I moan as he breathes hard against my neck and begins to move faster. "Go bigger now, Ori, to what you were before."

"Yes, Anne," he replies with a choked voice.

He lifts his head to kiss me again. I can feel him swelling inside me, the sudden increase in friction making us both groan low in our throats.

He breaks the kiss and pulls my hair back, giving me a desperate look. "I can feel your pulse around me. It's as if your heart beats only for the swell of my cock."

"Faster, Ori," I beg, my voice a high whine.

"Happy to oblige, my sweet." Ori hooks my legs over his arms and pumps faster, making me shout.

"Bigger now. And deeper. And *fuck*—go harder," I cry out.

I don't know if I can handle it but *I want it*.

Ori doesn't answer in words, he just growls before tossing my legs over his shoulders, making me yelp in surprise. In this position he's deeper, thrusts hard and fast. His cock swells much bigger than before. Almost too big.

But I don't want him to stop. It hurts, but the manic look in his eyes, the way he grits his teeth, his hair falling over his brow, is too beautiful to interrupt.

"Touch yourself, Anne," he barks out in a command. It's so unlike what I've seen from him so far, so… *alpha* I can't help but comply.

I circle my clit between the two of us as he relentlessly thrusts into me. I arch into him and cry out.

"Oh fuck, it's too much," I yell.

"No, it's not. Come for me, Anne. Now."

Once again, his command is one that must be met. I clench around him with a silent scream. I've never had an orgasm this hard. I squeeze so tight around Ori he grunts, his rhythm briefly faltering. I'm coming so hard I can't even make a sound; my mouth hangs open while my body is one tense statue. When, finally, the orgasm ends, I gasp loudly, throwing my hands over my head as I watch the point where our centers meet.

"You're not done, Anne," Ori growls. "I remember the things you like to watch. I remember the tentacles."

"What?" I am wholly unable to grasp what Ori is saying.

He's still sliding in and out of me, albeit more slowly than before, and it's all I can focus on.

"What does the hentai have to do with this?"

"Everything, Anne." Ori presses a hard kiss against my throat, licking and sucking hard enough to surely leave a mark.

I moan, running my fingers through the back of his hair as he kisses me, rocking my hips against his as he moves. It feels good, wonderful, and then it feels like…tentacles.

There are tentacles touching my vagina.

"Ori? What are you doing?" I squeal as one tentacle rubs against my already overly sensitized, slippery clit.

"Anything you want, Anne. Remember always that I can be anything you want me to be."

Ori pulls back far enough to gaze at the point of our lovemaking, a crazed look crossing his perfectly created features. A second thin tentacle slips alongside Ori's cock, stretching me, and I cry out in perfect agony.

"I will always give you everything you want even when you don't know you want it."

A third tentacle nudges against my rear entrance unexpectedly and I flinch. After a few breaths, I relax and decide that if I am going to be a tentacle fucker, then I might as go all the way.

Come on in, the backdoor's open!

The feeling of the first tentacle rubbing my clit combined with the second pressed against his cock inside my hot channel is already so intense. When that third one works its way into my tight asshole, I just explode.

I am rubbed, rutted, worked on, and writhed against and it's beyond overwhelming. Ori groans as I squeeze, pulse, and shudder through my climax. His eyes can't stop flitting back and forth between my face and the place where he's fucking me. I finally manage to lift myself enough to look at what's going on down there and catch a glimpse of the tentacle rubbing my clit.

It's white, and smooth, and fuck *it's so weird, right*? But *damn* it feels good.

Suddenly the tentacles snap out of existence, or absorb back into his body, I'm not really sure. All I know is they're gone fast. I yelp with surprise. I'm left with my beautiful Ori, and his made-to-order cock. He kisses me deeply, running his fingers through my hair over and over before pulling back and rutting hard into me.

"*Oh*, Anne," Ori chokes out. "I'm going to come."

"Then come, please, fill me up."

I'm assuming he can't get me pregnant, so the whole breeding kink thing will be alright, right?

"You don't understand." His face screws up and he

pulls out of me with a hiss, holding his cock above me.

Okay, coming on my chest is fine too. I close my eyes and wait for the onslaught of jizz...but it doesn't come.

When I hear him gasp and moan my name, I cautiously open my eyes. Something tickles my stomach and I give an incredulous snort as I see the white, fluffy things in the air.

I lift my head to see a final spurt of downy feathers float out from the end of his cock. They're everywhere in the air between us, landing on my nude body, my face, my hair.

I begin to laugh; I can't control it.

The blissed-out look on Ori's face falls at the sound of my laughter. *Oh no.* He slides backward on the bed, away from me.

"No, no, I'm not laughing at you. Come here, please." I hold out my arms and wait, hoping he isn't too upset.

After a moment his look softens and he settles into my arms, head on my shoulder. "You promise you don't think I'm disgusting? I didn't think about what would happen until I was nearly there and then it hit me. All that's inside me that would come out are feathers."

"Disgusting? How could I think you're disgusting?

The feathers are so sweet! I laughed because of how much joy it brought me, not because I was making fun of you or something." I rub my face into his hair. "It's just another way you're perfect for me. It means you can never get me pregnant and since I absolutely do not want to ever get knocked-up that's like a huge plus."

I nip his ear and he laughs before settling his head on my chest.

"You're in charge of sweeping up all the mess though."

"Gladly. If a bit of housework is the only sacrifice I need to make to make love to the most beautiful woman on the planet, then so be it."

"You know, you haven't really met any other women."

"I don't need to. I've seen them on the internet when you're browsing it."

"Oh boy. You have a lot to learn. What am I going to do with you?" I ruffle his hair and giggle, thinking of all the things I'm going to have to teach him.

"Well, hopefully more sex. And you'll need to take me to buy at least one more pillow, as a replacement you know, since you're one short. For me to use, not you. You have me."

I roll my eyes. "Okay, Ori. Let's get a little rest and after that we'll learn about the world beyond the internet."

Chapter 16

Ori

"And this is a kitten. Personally, my pet of choice. They're just so fuzzy-wuzzy."

My Anne and I are at the animal rescue shelter picking out a pet. She's wanted one for a while, and I need company while she's at work, so we think a pet might be good for us.

I'm not quite at the social level to venture into the world on my own for long periods of time yet so I'm stuck at home without Anne during the day. I really don't mind; it's not as if that wasn't my reality for my entire existence prior to becoming a man. It will be nice to have another living being around though, I will admit. I have a great urge to serve and care for Anne, as she's the whole reason I'm alive. When she's not around, it will be good to use some of that energy to take care of a being that was abandoned and needs it desperately.

"Here, you hold the kitty." Anne passes the wriggling kitten to me, and I wrap it in my arms.

It really is a wonderful creature, so soft and full of

life. I scratch the top of its tiny gray head and it vibrates with a purr. My face cracks wide in a smile. The kitten kneads my arm until its claw catches on my fabric and tears a small hole. I don't bleed but a small puff of feathers floats through the air. The kitten sits up to bat at them.

I quickly hand the feline back to Anne, who looks around the room to make sure no one has seen what just happened. Thankfully no one has.

"Well, perhaps we should get a hamster instead. Or a fish."

I feel bad, crushing her kitten dreams. But Anne simply laughs.

"It's alright Ori, I think fish are pretty cool, too."

The next day we finished setting up our goldfish. Anne goes to work. The sweet little swimmer was a great choice. It's a lovely fish, and we picked a great big tank, so it has a lot of room to swim around. Apparently the person who had the fish before us kept it in a tiny bowl, which is quite sad, so I'm glad to give it a new life.

A knock on the door startles me, interrupting my enjoyment of Carl, which is what we named the fish.

I open the door and find none other than the landlord, an absolute asshole. He's been bothering Anne about me staying at the apartment, and finally forced her to pay extra for me to stay here. I have no idea what he wants now.

"Yes, James?" I drawl.

"I've said twenty times now, it's Jimmy. Just checking on the place, seeing you ain't got no more people staying here." He looks past me into the apartment.

"I assure you we have no one else here. Have a fine day now." I move to close the door, but *Jimmy* puts his Croc-wearing foot in the way.

"Not so fast. I see you got a pet now. That means a pet fee. That's a pet deposit plus pet rent each month." He grins as he scratches a sweaty armpit. "Gonna need that right away, fancy boy."

"It's a fish, *Jimmy*. I'm sure you don't need all of that." I say through clenched teeth.

Jimmy pushes past me into the apartment and I can feel a hot rage burning in my chest.

"Well, if you got a fish you might have something else. Let's see. You got a dog? A cat? Cat fee is extra seeing as they stink up the place and all."

He starts to head toward the bedroom. *Absolutely not.*

I take a step to follow him, but my leg gives out.

Damn it!

I haven't told Anne yet, but it appears I need to feed to keep up my life force. Those first times weren't enough; I need regular maintenance. I can't eat *food*, we've discovered, unfortunately, so that's no help. I need to drain life. I've been carefully skimming tiny bits from rude people when we've gone out without telling Anne, but everyone has been so pleasant lately. *Fuck.*

I rub my leg until I can limp along enough behind the landlord. By this time, he's made it to Anne's room and is bent over, searching under her bed.

"I don't see no cat but that don't mean you won't get one, so I'll be back soon," he says as he stands up.

I grab him by his thick, sweaty throat.

"I don't believe you will, James. I don't believe you'll bother me or my precious Anne ever again."

I begin to drain his life force slowly, relishing the feel of taking revenge on this parasite. I watch as he turns gray, feel my leg become stronger as he does. Before I am able to take all his life I stop, letting go of his throat. He falls, but I catch his limp form.

"No, you won't be coming back, will you?" I smile, pinching his sagging cheek.

As I leave the apartment I check to make sure the stairwell is empty, then carry James to the bottom of the stairs, where I leave him seated, drooling, propped carefully so he won't fall. Someone will find him eventually and take him somewhere safe, I'm sure.

I return to the apartment and watch Carl again, happily swimming in his big tank. I feel a strange sensation on my wrist and lift my sleeve to see what's going on. *Oh no.*

Flesh. Real flesh.

It appears I took too much life force and started to become more *man* than pillow. This simply won't do. Anne won't like this one bit. I run to the bedroom and remove my clothes, checking in the mirror to see if any other parts of me have turned to flesh. Thankfully there aren't any. I sigh in relief.

When Anne returns I carefully avoid letting her touch that particular area on my wrist. It will take a while for my life energy to fade down enough for that to go away but I'm sure it will. For now, I'll just be careful she doesn't touch it.

As for James, he was gone when she arrived, and no one came knocking at our door to ask any questions. Perfect.

"Darling, are you hungry? Do you want me to order you some tacos? Curry?" I ask my sweet Anne as I rub her feet.

She had a tough day at work, and I want to make sure she's as comfortable at home as she can be.

"Oh no, I'm good. I had some pizza at work for some dumb pizza party they threw as a bonus instead of actually giving us a raise. So, I'm stuffed."

My lip quirks up at the side. I lean back on our new pillow, one stuffed with artificial material—I don't trust feathers—and grin broadly at my Anne.

"Actually, I believe I'm the one that's stuffed."

Thank you to Latrexa, Vera, Tawny, Shannon, and everyone else who helped make this story possible. You are the best of people, flesh or fabric.

Printed in Great Britain
by Amazon

32397900R00046